Bad River Boys

A Meeting of the Lakota Sioux with Lewis and Clark

BY VIRGINIA
DRIVING HAWK SNEVE

ILLUSTRATIONS BY
BILL FARNSWORTH

Holiday House / New York

"*Hoka Hey!*" Cloud shouted.

"*Yiii-yah!*" shrilled Sun.

"Wait!" cried Antler, struggling to shinny onto his horse. But the older boys were already racing their steeds to the shore of the Wakpa Sica, the Bad River. The boys clung to the manes of the hard-pounding steeds, and then came to a shuddering halt.

The boys laughed and looked over their family's herd of horses. The setting sun sent golden rays across the sluggish river.

"Cloud," Antler called to his brother. "Look."

Cloud peered out at the river. "It is a boat but not Truteau's."

Truteau, a French trader, was a friend to the tribe. It was exciting when he brought them guns, kettles, woven blankets, mirrors, cloth, whisky, and *skuya*, or sweets.

"Let's swim over to greet the *wasicus*, white men," said Cloud.

"We can't leave the herd for too long," Antler cautioned, following the older boys.

They were good swimmers and soon reached the large boat.

"*Ho*!" Cloud called, treading water. He was startled by a low growl, and a voice that snapped an order in a language that he did not understand. It was not Lakota or French. The boat rocked, and gun barrels poked over its side. A dog barked and was quickly hushed.

"Who are you?" the voice growled again. This time Cloud understood the question.

"Sun, Antler, and Cloud," he answered as he signed to the younger boys, *Be ready to swim underwater!*

"Of what tribe?"

"Sicangu, of Black Buffalo's band."

The men on the boat conferred. Then the interpreter said, "Come closer."

The three swam to the boat, and in the remaining light the white men saw that they were only boys. They lowered their guns. "Is your village near?"

"*Hanh*, yes." Cloud tried to raise an arm to point to the opposite shore but he was too tired from treading water. "There are two villages with furs to trade. May we come on your boat?"

The boys were pulled aboard and rowed to the west shore.

"Tell your chiefs they must come to meet with us tomorrow," the interpreter said.

"*Skuya?*" Antler asked. He loved the sweets traders usually brought.

No! was the answer as the boys climbed from the boat.

The boys quickly found their
mounts and drove the herd to
the night pasture. Antler
and Sun stayed to
hobble each horse
with short ropes on
their front legs to keep
them from straying too far
in the night. Cloud raced into
the village, creating an uproar.

"Cloud," the boy's father, Black
Buffalo, called. "What is wrong?"

Cloud explained, as Sun and Antler
returned from the pasture. Black Buffalo and
the elders conferred, then sent five warriors to
survey the white men's boat before dark.

"Go to your mothers," he told them. "You have done well
enough for this day."

Reluctantly, but also pleased to be praised, the boys obeyed.
The mothers were full of questions and the boys told their story
again.

"*Hinh!*"the women cried. "You could have been shot."

Cloud and Antler's mother, True Woman, told Cloud, "You must not lead your
younger brother into danger. You must also keep Sun safe. His mother, Shell,
could not bear to lose him!"

The next morning Black Buffalo and his fellow chiefs sat in council with other men to discuss the strangers. The boys told what had happened the day before.

"They are dangerous if they threaten children!" Low murmurs of agreement came from the men.

The five warriors then reported. "The old Frenchman who speaks for them does not know our language well. We do not understand what they want. Nor do we know if he translates our words correctly," said one warrior.

"The Frenchman did not listen," another added. "He kept talking. He said the whites were our friends and wanted to continue to be so."

"They pointed guns at us, and we left. They want to meet with our chiefs on the island in the river they call Teton but we call Wakpa Sica."

"What do these men call themselves?" asked Black Buffalo.

"Americans."

Now the murmur of the council was loud as the men discussed this news.

"Are these the Americans the Yankton spoke of?" asked one.

The tribe had seen the Yankton in the early summer at the Dakota Rendezvous. Every year the Sicangu and other Sioux tribes gathered to feast, dance, renew friendships, visit relatives, and trade at a place on the Wakpakin. There the Sicangu traded hides and pelts with the Sisseton and Yankton Sioux for kettles and other metal items these tribes got from white posts in the East. The Sicangu then traded these goods for farm produce and horses with the Arikara farmers upstream. No traders traveling up the river were allowed to trade directly with the Arikara unless they first offered gifts to the Sicangu.

At the Rendezvous, the Sisseton had traded their British flags for the Sicangu's Spanish and French flags. The flags were favored decorations for a chief's lodge.

The Yankton told of Americans coming to their villages. The council was wary of these American strangers who came with guns but no gifts. Black Buffalo said, "Have the women pack in case they must take the children and old ones to safety."

Cloud, Sun, and Antler were told to move the horses farther away from the river. The villagers scattered to prepare for the Americans.

When the boys awoke the next day, their mothers kept a close watch on them. They insisted that each one's hair be combed and newly braided.

"The council with the white men will be on the large sandbar in the Wakpa Sica," Sun's mother reported.

Cloud had to be patient as True Woman tugged on his hair and warned, "Do not do anything foolish today. We don't know what these strangers want."

"*Hanh, Ina,*" Cloud responded, and raced away.

The boys met near a willow tree and watched the chiefs Black Buffalo, Partisan, and Black Medicine canoe to the island while warriors followed in bullboats.

They waited a long time for something to happen.

Finally Cloud's mother and other women filled a bullboat with fat buffalo roasts. There would be no trouble as long as there was feasting at the council.

The three boys lingered, and the warriors told them to climb onto the highest branches of a tree to get a better view of the meeting.

"Tell us what you see," the warriors said.

"The white men are marching together—all the same clothing. They follow one who carries their flag."

"Look," cried Antler. "One white man is *hesapa!*"

"*Hanh,*" agreed Cloud. "A black man."

"Is that *mato,*" asked Sun. "A bear?"

The boys stared at a large, dark, furry shape sitting by a white man. It stood, wagged its tail, and barked.

"*Shunka!*" they exclaimed. "A dog!"

The boys clung to the swaying branches as several warriors climbed for a firsthand view. None of the Sicangu had ever seen a black man or such a huge dog.

"He is giving gifts to our chiefs," said Antler. They could see that Black Buffalo had a red coat and an odd thing on his head. Partisan and Black Medicine were each handed something the watchers could not identify.

They heard Partisan complain that the Americans had slighted him and Black Medicine. Their gifts were paltry things compared to what Black Buffalo had received.

Partisan demanded that the strangers stay with the Sicangu or leave a pirogue full of trade goods before they could move upstream. The Americans refused. There was much shouting and stomping about on the sandbar. Then suddenly there was a puff of smoke and a roar of thunder as the men on the boat fired a gun in the air. The warriors onshore grabbed for their weapons.

The spectators could not see what was happening and worried about the safety of their chiefs. Finally the Americans rowed the chiefs back to shore in a pirogue.

Partisan's warriors rushed to the landing and seized the pirogue's bow cable. One warrior wrapped his arms around the boat's short mast. Chief Partisan spoke to the Americans. "Your boat cannot go!"

One of the Americans pulled a long knife. From high in the tree the boys saw a gun barrel aim at the shore. At Black Buffalo's signal, the women and children began moving toward the village. Black Buffalo jerked the boat cable from the warriors and ordered them away from the boat. The warriors strung their bows and took arrows from their quivers. Tensely, they waited for the signal to attack.

Black Buffalo and the American shouted at each other. The angry words lost much of their impact and meaning after being translated by the old Frenchman.

"We will go on!" demanded the American. "My men are not squaws but warriors!"

Black Buffalo declared, "Our warriors will follow and kill all of you."

The American shouted back, but the nervous Frenchman quietly said, "We have been sent by our Chief of the Seventeen Fires. He can summon more warriors in a moment to punish all. . . ."

"Look," whispered Sun, and pointed to a fast-approaching canoe filled with American soldiers.

The warriors fitted arrows to bows, but Black Buffalo waved them back.

Still gripping the pirogue's cable, he now stood alone with the white man.

SPLASH!

There was sudden quiet after Antler fell from the tree into the water.

Both men turned to look at the boy as he bobbed to the surface.

American soldiers lifted Antler into the boat. He tried to keep the big dog from licking his face.

"Seaman, no!" the white chief ordered.

No one laughed, but the incident had eased the tension. Black Buffalo nodded his thanks and spoke in a calmer tone: "Our women and children would like to visit your boat and see its wonderful things."

The American agreed. Black Buffalo dropped the cable and the pirogue swung into the river. "Our women and children are poor. We need trade goods. It is sad that you must leave so soon."

It was agreed that the next day the women and children could visit the keelboat and that the chiefs would sleep on the keelboat that night.

The soldiers went back to the boat. Black Buffalo assigned his warriors as sentries and sent the boys home.

The next morning, groups of women and children lined up to visit the boat.

The boys followed their mothers but stopped when they saw the big dog looking at them. The camp dogs they had seen were small, wiry curs. This one was almost as big and furry as a bear. It gave a low *Woof* and its tail thumped the deck.

Antler touched the dog, which tried to lick his face again. The other boys laughed and petted the dog. Time passed quickly and too soon the visit was over.

Back onshore, the women prepared a feast and dance to honor the Americans. Great chunks of buffalo roasted on skewers over hot coals. Corn and squash simmered in iron trade kettles.

At the feast the boys observed the visitors carefully. After the Sicangu chiefs were seated, three young warriors carried the first American chief, Lewis, on a beautifully painted buffalo hide. Next they brought the American with red hair.

The American chiefs gave Black Buffalo an American flag.

Black Buffalo rose and thanked the Americans for the gift. He urged them to stay. "To honor my people with your presence. We also have fine furs to trade."

The Frenchman spoke only a few words after the chief's long oration. Cloud wondered if the interpreter had said the right words, for the whites did not seem impressed.

The chief took up his pipe, pointed it to the sky, to each of the directions, and to the earth. He lit the pipe, blew smoke to the directions, and passed it to the guests. This was the greatest honor for the Americans, even if they did not understand.

When it was time to eat, the rest of the Americans sat in the large circle. Among them was the *hesapa,* called York. All of the villagers were awed by the big man. York, with the help of the Frenchman, told the Sicangu that he had once been a wild animal. But after he was caught, the American chief kept him as a slave.

"I am the strongest of all men!" he boasted, and to prove it he beckoned to Cloud, Sun, Antler, and three other boys. He had them grasp his forearms and lifted them off the ground. When two more boys were added, he hoisted them higher still so that their feet dangled. The spectators cheered and laughed as York shook his arms and the boys fell to the ground.

After the meal, the dancing began around a large fire in the center of the village. Hand drums pounded, and long sticks with dangling deer hooves rattled to the beat. Women, wearing their finest clothes, proudly showed their men's war trophies as they danced. Warriors told of courageous battle deeds, and all of the villagers danced to honor their bravery.

It was very late when the dancing stopped. The visitors rose and made their way to the shore. The weary boys went home and were soon asleep.

The next afternoon, Black Buffalo and the other chiefs escorted the white chiefs on a walk through the village. They again urged the Americans to stay and trade, explaining that farther north winter would soon keep them in its grip until spring. Here, buffalo was plentiful. But the Americans insisted they must go. They moved to the river and, followed by Partisan and one of his warriors, rowed to the keelboat.

CRASH!

The harsh noise reverberated over the water as the pirogue slammed into the keelboat's anchor cable. The cable broke, and the boats veered dangerously close to each other. The dog barked. The Americans shouted and rushed to stop the swinging boats from crashing.

"It's an attack!" cried someone onshore.

"It is the Omaha," cried another.

Alarmed warriors reached for their weapons and tensions rose until the Frenchman haltingly explained what had happened. Relieved, most of the men went back to the village, but Black Buffalo assigned many warriors to keep watch during the night. He still could not trust the white men.